Finally everything was taken out of the apartment, and we all went downstairs. I got into the van and sat on Papi's lap. He hugged me.

"Well, we're off to a better future, Felita," Papi whispered.

I didn't answer. In a little while my street would be filled with lots of people and kids playing. I would be someplace else and no longer part of them. I tried not to cry. After the truck pulled away and turned the corner, I leaned over and looked out the window. Our old neighborhood was far behind us.

———————

"Mohr scores with her first story for younger readers, capturing the spirit of family and neighborhood."

—*School Library Journal*

"This story by award-winning Mohr is as vivid a book as *El Bronx Remembered* and her other exceptional works. Cruz's pictures portray all the doings vividly."

—*Publishers Weekly*

·FELITA·

by *Nicholasa Mohr*
pictures by Ray Cruz

A BANTAM SKYLARK BOOK®
NEW YORK · TORONTO · LONDON · SYDNEY · AUCKLAND

ABOUT THE AUTHOR

Nicholasa Mohr began her career as a graphic artist before she decided to devote herself to writing full time. Her award-winning books include *In Nueva York, El Bronx Remembered,* and *Going Home,* the sequel to *Felita.* Nicholasa Mohr was born in New York City's El Barrio and now lives in Brooklyn, New York.

ABOUT THE ILLUSTRATOR

Ray Cruz has illustrated many children's books, among them *Alexander and the Terrible, Horrible, No Good, Very Bad Day* and *How the Moolah Was Taught a Lesson.* He lives in New York City.

RL 4, 007–011

*This edition contains the complete text
of the original hardcover edition.*
NOT ONE WORD HAS BEEN OMITTED.

FELITA
*A Bantam Skylark Book / published by arrangement with
Dial Books*

Printing History
Dial Books edition published 1979
Bantam edition / April 1990
*Skylark Books is a registered trademark of Bantam Books, a division of
Bantam Doubleday Dell Publishing Group, Inc. Registered in U.S. Patent
and Trademark Office and elsewhere.*

*Bantam Books are published by Bantam Books, a division of Bantam
Doubleday Dell Publishing Group, Inc. Its trademark, consisting of the
words "Bantam Books" and the portrayal of a rooster, is Registered in U.S.
Patent and Trademark Office and in other countries, Marca Registrada.
Bantam Books, 666 Fifth Avenue, New York, New York 10103.*

PRINTED IN THE UNITED STATES OF AMERICA

OPM   0 9 8 7 6 5 4 3

• For Elsie, my dear sister •

Contents

•FELITA•

• one •

The Last Day

Right up till that very moment I didn't believe it
would really happen. But suddenly there I was sur-
rounded by boxes and cartons packed tightly with just
about everything we owned. All morning long we
had been working, filling up these boxes and cartons.
In fact Papi, and Tito and Johnny, my two brothers,
had gone out to find more boxes and buy rope and
sealing tape. Even though Mami, Papi, and everybody
had spoken of practically nothing else for the past

month, I had just kept thinking that moving day was still a long way off. But today was our last day: Tomorrow we would be moving into a brand-new neighborhood. The worst part of it was leaving all my friends and my block. I didn't remember ever living any place else. That's because, as Mami said, I was only a baby and couldn't even talk when we moved to this apartment and this neighborhood.

I looked up at the huge blank space staring at me over the living-room couch. Mami's brightly colored tapestry of the Last Supper, showing Jesus and the apostles seated around a long table set with loaves of bread and whole fish, was gone. That tapestry was Mami's favorite piece in the apartment. She and Papi had bought it when they had set up house as newlyweds.

"It was the first luxury we permitted ourselves in our very own apartment," she had explained. When people admired it, Mami felt proud. Now that it was packed away too, I knew it was official, and we didn't live here anymore.

"Felita! Felita . . . what are you doing?"

"I'm just thinking, Mami."

"Come on now, don't look so grumpy. You'll see,

you are gonna like the new neighborhood." There she was, smiling again. Acting like nothing bad was happening. It made no sense to talk to her.

"I'm going out to play, Mami. I promised Gigi, Paquito, and Consuela I would meet them down by the stoop."

"Felita, you know we still have lots to do. Especially today."

"Please, please, Mami! This is my last day to be with my friends and I already promised to meet them . . ."

"All right, Felita. But only for a little while and then you plan to get back here and help. Understand? Your father and brothers can't do it all. Besides, Papi might be working tonight at the plant. We need the money, so he'll take overtime, if he can get it. That means we still have lots to pack and you have responsibilities here."

I ran out as fast as I could. Was I glad to get away from her and all that packing! I looked around outside. Boy, I loved my block. I knew just about everybody on this street. I could stroll along and say hello to somebody practically every minute. I saw my friends walking toward me.

"Hey! Felita, over here!" There was Paquito with

Consuela and her little sister, Joanie. Consuela always had to mind Joanie. Like it or not, when Consuela was there, so was Joanie.

"Where's Gigi?" asked Consuela.

"She's supposed to meet us here. But let's go down to the cheaperia store and shop around. I told Gigi that's where we would all be in case we didn't wait for her."

We walked down to the cheaperia store. Everybody called it this because you could buy anything there real cheap. The sign outside read: GOLDSTEIN'S HOUSE-HOLD MART—NEW AND USED BARGAINS.

Mr. Goldstein wasn't around anymore. Mr. Perez was the owner. He was nice and didn't mind when we just looked around and didn't buy. You could buy secondhand toys there. Once I bought a used jump rope. It looked new, with shiny red wooden handles. I shared it with Gigi. We shared everything. Grown-ups could buy pots and pans, even clothing, in this store. Today we were checking if there might be a yellow party dress for sale.

In just two weeks Gigi was having her birthday party. She was going to be nine years old. Gigi is older than me by five months. We had planned to wear the exact same kind of dress—this way we could look just like sisters. Gigi is an only child, and I have two older brothers. That's why, when Gigi and I were little, we decided to become sisters. Consuela has three older sisters, and Paquito comes from a large family. He has five sisters and three brothers. Paquito was somewhere in the middle. Even though all of us are really tight, and good friends, everyone knows how Gigi and I feel about each other.

I was really disappointed when Mami told me I couldn't have a new dress for the party. It was all on account of that dumb move that we couldn't afford it. Gigi's dress was so pretty. It was a bright yellow, made of soft silky material, with a lace collar and velvet trimming. Our only hope was to look around in the cheaperia store. All my friends agreed to chip in and help me buy a dress if we got lucky and found one.

"Felita, Consuela, Paquito!" We turned around. There was Gigi. "Did you find it?" she asked.

"Not yet," I answered.

"The stuff here ain't so good," said Paquito.

"Let's look some more anyway," Gigi responded.

We carefully inspected the racks filled with used clothing. Most of the clothes weren't even pretty or new looking. Some of them needed washing and mending.

"You find something you like?" Mr. Perez asked. He was chewing on his cigar. He always had an unlit half-smoked cigar in his mouth. When he spoke, it remained clenched tightly between his teeth.

"No, not today," I answered.

"Well, you try again, yes?"

"Sure," I answered. Well, that was that! I wouldn't be shopping here again. I felt miserable. Not only wouldn't I be living on the block when Gigi had her party, but I wasn't getting my dress either. Gigi put her arm around my shoulder.

"Come on, Felita," she said, "let's hang out." I could see she was feeling pretty bad herself.

We all headed back to my stoop. As we passed by Doña Josefina's bodega we heard her call out.

"Felita, you moving today or tomorrow?" She was standing at the entrance, looking at me.

"Tomorrow, Doña Josefina."

"Well, don't look so sad, eh? I heard you going to live in a better neighborhood."

"I guess so." I shrugged.

"Don't forget to come by later with your mother and say goodbye." Doña Josefina bent over toward me and winked. "I got a little special treat for you. I give it to you later, eh?" That sure didn't sound like her.

Usually she was telling us not to touch anything. She always watched to make sure we didn't swipe some of her delicious candy. Dulce de coco, coconut candy. White, crunchy, sweet, and so delicious! Doña Josefina made it herself. She set it out on the counter in large trays. I hoped it was some of that candy she was going to give me. Oh, man . . . I could already taste it melting in my mouth! I was planning to come by later with Mami, all right.

Renaldo's Record and TV Radio Repair Shop was blasting out a loud and fast number. Right away Joanie began to dance. Shaking, turning, and stepping, right there on the sidewalk. People standing around began to laugh; others stopped just to watch her. Joanie is a terrific show-off. She knows she can get away with all that carrying on because she's only five.

"Isn't she cute!" a lady said.

"Look . . . mira, qué linda! She's so pretty, and can she dance!" A man smiled, nodding at everyone.

When Joanie acted like this, I mostly got embarrassed and walked away. But now, looking at her and knowing that I wasn't going to be around much longer, I had to admit she was a cute kid after all.

It was getting late and I realized I would have to

get back upstairs. I didn't want to think about to-morrow . . . that I was not going to be hanging out with my friends on my block. As we walked along I looked inside Wong's laundry, where Mami sent Papi's shirts sometimes. Maybe I should say goodbye to them. Mrs. Wong was busy working and Mr. Wong wasn't around. I decided to keep going. Bernie's candy store was empty except for Old Bernie, who was sitting reading the paper and petting his cat as usual. I wished at that very moment I could treat us all to something, but even though I had taken every cent I had with me on account of the dress, I still didn't have enough money.

We reached my stoop and sat down. Everyone was real quiet.

"Hey," I said, breaking the silence. "You are all coming to visit me in our new apartment. Even you, Joanie. Consuela, you can bring her."

"When?" Joanie jumped up and down.

"Real soon. Just as soon as we get settled there."

"What you kids doing here?" someone yelled. I saw Tito waving at us. He and Johnny were coming up the block carrying some cartons and packages. "Felita," Tito continued, "you're supposed to be working, not goofing off. Right, Johnny?"

"I was working! And you know it. Mami gave me permission to play outside for a little while."

"Yeah, sure," Tito responded. "I'll bet she didn't."

"She did too!" Sometimes Tito could be a terrible pest.

"You better be upstairs, girl, before you get it." Tito put down his bundles and made a gesture as if he were going to smack me. "Like this . . ." He swung in my direction.

"Johnny!" I screamed. "Tell him to stop it." I couldn't stand that silly Tito, especially today.

"All right," Johnny said, "leave her alone." Johnny was the oldest and my favorite. Johnny is thirteen and a half, and Tito is twelve. Johnny looks just like Mami. He has light-brown skin and short black curly hair. Tito looks like Papi. He is blond and has very pale pink skin.

Mami was always telling Papi, "God gave you one child and me another, but Felita, she belongs to both of us." That was because I look like a mixture of Mami and Papi.

"Johnny, I was just telling my friends they could come to visit us at our new place, right?" I asked.

"Sure, it ain't far. You could walk there," Johnny said. "It will take about twenty minutes if you go fast

and half an hour if you take your time. By bus it's
only, like, five minutes."

"Great," Paquito said.

"Fantastic." Gigi smiled.

"Listen," Tito said. "We'll be coming back to visit
the block. After all I got all my friends here. So you
know you'll be seeing my face. In fact it's a big drag
having to go someplace else and trying to make new
friends again."

"Don't you wanna move?" asked Paquito.

"No way," Tito answered. "It ain't us . . . it's our
parents who want to leave. Right, Johnny, Felita?"
Johnny and I nodded in agreement.

"Everybody says you are all moving into a way
better neighborhood," said Paquito.

"I suppose that's so," said Johnny. "But we are sure
gonna miss everybody."

"There are no Ricans where we're going," said Tito.

"Who lives there?" asked Consuela.

"Mostly Irish and German people, something like
that," Johnny said. "At least that's the way it looked
to me."

"Mostly gringos, that's who," Tito said.

"Well, you look like a gringo yourself," said Consuela, "so you should be right at home."

"I may look like a gringo, but I'm Puerto Rican. And them that don't like it can shove it."

"Where?" asked Paquito.

"Way down yonder in their beehives!"

Everyone laughed.

"Felita! Felita!"

I could hear Mami's voice. I looked up and there she was, looking down at us from our window.

"Mira! All of you, it's time to get up here. Now!"

"I gotta go," I said.

"Don't forget," said Gigi, "you will be coming to my party. And maybe you can stay overnight."

"That would be great. I'll ask Mami. Anyway I'll be at that party. Nobody could ever keep me away."

"We'll see you soon," Paquito said.

"At your new house, right?" asked Consuela.

"Me too, me too!" Joanie giggled.

My brothers went on ahead of me taking their packages and cartons. I put on a great big smile. "See you guys." I ran up the stoop steps and headed upstairs.

A sinking feeling was making me feel sick inside. I could hardly climb the two flights of stairs. Each step was taking me farther away from my friends. It wasn't fair, nobody had asked me if I wanted to move. Anytime one of us kids complained, Papi would always say the same thing: "It's for better schools. You children will thank us."

Tito always spoke his mind, but Johnny was different. He was quiet by nature. Maybe that's why Papi always tried to reason with him: "Johnny, you are the oldest, so you must be the one to understand and set a good example for your brother and sister. Think of your future and theirs. You will go to a better high school from that neighborhood and then college."

Johnny is real smart. He's best in math. Someday, Papi and Mami say, Johnny is going to be a scientist or something very special. Tito is smart too, but not like Johnny. Tito likes to goof off and hang out too much. Papi said that Tito needs a good school more than anybody else because he needs the discipline.

I finally reached my floor and went into the apartment. I heard Mami's voice.

"Felita, what took you so long? I thought you were never getting up here!" Mami was sorting out some clothes. "Now your father is coming back soon with some very large cartons. We have to make room. Let's start labeling and putting aside these boxes that are already packed."

I began to work alongside Mami, sealing boxes. I wondered what our new apartment would look like.

I had seen the new neighborhood and the building, but I had never been inside.

"Mami, what's our new place look like?" I asked.

"It looks something like this apartment. Except it's laid out a little different and we've got a much larger and nicer kitchen. You'll like it. Wait. You'll be as pleased as I am."

Early the next morning, after breakfast, I looked out the front window. Most people were still indoors and the street was quiet. Everybody was rushing around me. Mami was arguing with the moving men.

"That's my good dishes. You be careful! Be careful! Don't drop that box, whatever you do."

Papi was helping the moving men take down the large furniture. He was really working up a sweat. His shirt was all wet and stuck to his skin. Papi is very strong. He works at a big food plant way downtown. He repairs heavy machinery there. Everytime there is trouble with equipment, Papi has to repair it.

"Felita!" Mami called out. "What are you doing standing about with your mouth open? Catching flies? Please help. Make sure everything in your room is packed away."

Quickly I went into my old room. Everything was disappearing rapidly. My bed and chair were already gone. I started stuffing some crayons, the socks I found on the floor, and other odds and ends into boxes.

Finally everything was taken out of the apartment, and we all went downstairs. Papi promised me I could ride in the moving van with him. Mami and my brothers were taking the bus. I looked at the quiet street and glanced over at Doña Josefina's. I hadn't gone by to see her with Mami last night like she asked. Her store was open, but I still wasn't going over. As much as I loved that dulce de coco, I wasn't in the mood. I got into the van and sat on Papi's lap. He hugged me.

"Well, we're off to a better future, Felita," Papi whispered.

I didn't answer. In a little while my street would be filled with lots of people and kids playing. I would be someplace else and no longer part of them. I tried not to cry. After the truck pulled away and turned the corner, I leaned over and looked out the window. Our old neighborhood was far behind us.

• two •

Trouble

The new apartment was almost the same size as our old one. There was a living room, kitchen, bathroom, small dining room, and two bedrooms. I was given the dining room for my room. My brothers shared a bedroom and my parents got the master bedroom. One nice thing about our new home was that we had a large kitchen, as Mami had said. This really pleased her. She was busy making new curtains, matching appliance covers, and place mats. We had been here almost a full week now, and although boxes still had to be unpacked, the big furniture was already set in place. Also we had to climb one more floor. We now lived on the third floor facing front.

I stood by the living-room window looking out. The day was warm and sunny. Below on the sidewalk a group of girls were playing rope—double dutch. Some of them were real good. This block was different from my old street. There were hardly any small stores except for Maloney's Food Center and Davenport's Antiques and Secondhand Furniture Shop. The street was cleaner and quieter. There were not as many people or kids outside.

"Go out and play, Felita. Why don't you go out and make friends? It's such nice weather. Go on, honey." Mami kept telling me this every day.

"I don't feel well, Mami. Maybe tomorrow." I really felt fine. I was just scared to go out into that new block with all those strange kids.

"Mira . . . look here, Felita, we have been in this place for a week now, and you still haven't been out to play. What's wrong?"

"I don't know anybody here, Mami."

"And you will never know anybody here either if you stay indoors. Mi hijita, please, por favor, give the children a chance to know you. Tito and Johnny go out."

"Sure, they are big, Mami. They can travel to our old block. You won't let me travel alone."

"Stop being silly. You are too young to go traveling alone. Never mind. Guess what I bought you?"

"What, Mami?"

"This dress. Look, it's like a sailor's suit."

I wished it had been the yellow party dress I wanted. Still, it was pretty. It had a white top and a dark-blue pleated skirt.

"Thanks, Mami."

"I was saving it for school," Mami said, "but I think it would be nice for you to have something new to wear on the first day you go out to meet our new neighbors. Yes? What do you say, Felita?"

"All right, Mami."

Mami polished my white shoes, and brushed my dark hair until it gleamed. I put on my dress and looked in the mirror. I looked nice, even pretty.

"Mami, can we ever move back to our neighborhood? I want to be with my friends again."

"Felita, this neighborhood has better schools. You and your brothers will get a good education. But yes, we will visit the old neighborhood. After all, Abuelita, your grandmother, still lives there, and your Tío Jorge too. Besides, we will have our friends come to our new home. Please try to understand, honey."

"Okay, Mami."

"Now be friendly. Remember, you will make good friends here."

I stood on the stoop, watching the group of girls I had seen from my window. They had stopped playing rope and were now playing hopscotch. One of them saw me, then whispered to the others. They all stopped playing and looked at me. I made sure to turn in the other direction. Slowly I went down the steps to the sidewalk and leaned against the stoop railing. Then I walked toward them and stood only a few feet away. They were having a good time, using bottle caps and keys to toss on the chalked squares. Hopscotch was one game I was really good at!

"Hi! Hey you!" a girl with short brown hair and glasses wearing blue jeans called out. "You wanna play with us?"

"Sure." I walked over and waited my turn. There were six of them playing. They were all about my age. They played a fair game of hopscotch. One girl with bright carrot-colored hair and lots of freckles was the best. But she wasn't as good as me. At last my turn came. I did the whole ten boxes forward and backward without one mistake.

"You're real good," one of the girls said.

"Even better than Molly." The girl with the glasses pointed to the girl with the bright hair and freckles. "What's your name?" she asked.

"Felita."

"Wow," she said, "that's real pretty. My name is Katherine. This here is Molly . . . and Mary Beth, Wendy, Thelma, and Margaret Jean."

"You must of played hopscotch before," said Molly.

"I did. On my old block we played it a whole lot."

"Let's play some more," said Katherine.

We all played. When it was my turn, I got to play over and over because I was the best one. Molly was second best. Margaret Jean was the slowest and she hardly got a full turn because she kept stepping on the lines.

"After this," Margaret Jean said, "let's play some jump rope again."

We all agreed and played for a long time.

"Are you going to our school, Felita?" Katherine asked.

"I think so."

"What was the school you went to?" asked Wendy.

"Oh, P.S. 47. That was near our old neighborhood."

"Our school is P.S. 91. It's real near here," said Molly.

"I'm sure you will be going to our school," said Katherine. "Everybody in this neighborhood goes there. We walk together every morning. You wanna walk with us when school starts again?"

"That's neat. Thanks," I said. They were really nice. Maybe it wouldn't be so bad here after all.

"You know, sometimes we get together at each other's homes and have, like, a meeting," Wendy said. She was the tallest one and had two long straw-colored braids and bangs. "We might even form a club. It's not a sure thing yet. We have to plan it. Listen, would you like to come to our next meeting?"

"Sure. I would really like to come to your next meeting very much."

"You live in this building, right?" asked Katherine.

"On the third floor in front." I nodded.

"I live down the block in that house." She pointed to another gray brick building about midway down the street. "But Mary Beth and Thelma live in your building."

"I been living there all my life," said Mary Beth. "Thelma moved here when she was real little."

"We seen you move in," said Thelma.

"I was real little when I moved into my old block . . ." I said.

"I was four," Thelma said. "That's what my mother told me anyway."

"Mary Beth, what are you doing?" a woman called out. She stood with several men and women near my stoop.

"Playing, Mama."

"Get over here!"

"Wendy, Thelma, Molly . . . all of you, come here. Right now!"

All the girls walked over to the grown-ups except Katherine.

"I gotta be getting on home," she murmured and walked off.

The other girls huddled together with the grown-ups. They all spoke in low voices. I waited. Were they coming back to play? They all stared silently at me. I smiled at them and waited, but there were no smiles for me. I glanced up at our window, hoping that Mami might be watching. No one was there. I looked around at the unfamiliar street. Katherine had already disappeared into her building. Suddenly I felt frightened and all alone. I wanted to get home, upstairs, where I would be safe with Mami. I decided to head for my apartment. Now the adults and girls were standing in a group beside the stoop steps. As I approached my building I lowered my eyes and quickened my pace. I figured I would walk around them and get up the steps as fast as I could.

Thelma quickly stepped in front of me, blocking my way. "Why did you move here?"

"Why don't you stay with your own kind?" Mary Beth stood next to Thelma.

"Yeah, there's none of your kind here and we don't want you." As I tried to get by them the other three girls ran up the stoop and formed a line across the building entrance.

I turned toward the grown-ups. Some were smiling. Others looked angry.

"She should stay in her own place, right, Mama?"

"Can't you answer? No speak the English no more?" The grown-ups laughed.

". . . so many colors in your family. What are you?"

"Her mother is black and her father is white."

"They ain't white . . . just trying to pass!"

"Niggers."

"Shh, don't say that."

"All right, spicks. God only knows what they are!"

"Go on back to your own country."

"Let me through!" I screamed.

"Nobody's stopping you." Mary Beth and Thelma stepped aside. I took a deep breath, tried not to cry, walked up the stoop, and began to push past the other three girls blocking the entrance.

"Watch it!" They pushed back, shoving me down a couple of steps.

"Mami!" I looked up at the window. No one was there. "Let me go by!" I shouted.

I pushed again. I felt a sharp punch in my back and a fist hit the side of my face. Then a wall of arms came crashing down. I began to cry hard.

"Mami . . . Mamita . . ."

"Here now. That's enough!" a man said.

"Let her go," a woman shouted. "She knows now she's not wanted here. Girls, let her through."

As I ran past, someone pulled at my skirt and I heard it rip. I ran up three flights of stairs, crying until I was safe inside my apartment. I made sure the front door was bolted behind me. I ran right into Mami's arms.

"Felita, pero qué pasó? What happened?" Mami asked.

It took some time before I stopped crying and could talk clearly, making some sense to Mami. She patiently questioned me until I told her all that had happened.

"I hate them, Mami. I want them all to die! I would like to kill them back!" The concern in Mami's face changed to a knowing look, and she nodded.

Mami washed my face and gently kissed me.

"There, there, Felita, it's all right," she said. Mami sat me in her lap and rocked me until I calmed down. We were both silent for a long while.

"How about a treat? Chocolate milk, yes?" We went into the kitchen. I drank my milk and felt a little better.

"Felita, these are ignorant and foolish people, but I don't want you to hate them for that."

"They hit me, Mami, tore my dress. Look." I showed Mami the long tear at the back of my skirt. "See? They called us bad names. They said awful things. I do hate them, I do!"

"Mi hijita, my little daughter, listen to me. To stand up to them like you did was right. You were brave to push past all of them and get home safe. Wait until I tell Papi and your brothers. They will be so proud of you! Felita, you are special to us, your familia. But when you hate, it makes you feel bad inside and turns you mean, just like them. Understand, these people are wrong, but you must not hate them. Instead you must learn to love yourself. That is more important. To love yourself and feel worthy, despite anything they might say against you and your family! That is the real victory. It will make you strong inside. Do you understand, Felita?"

"I think so, Mami. But I'm still angry at them and I don't like them, not one bit! I would like to call them a lotta bad things . . . those dirty . . ."

"Shh, Felita, stop! Okay, I don't like them either. And I'm very, very angry at them. Bunch of stupid ignoramuses and bullies! But anger is not hate. Yes? I would like to see them try to pick on me. Oh, no, they have to pick on a defenseless child. Bunch of nasty fools is what they are."

"Maybe we could go down right now and tell them off, Mami."

"No, it's not worth it. Best to ignore them. I don't want to start trouble, honey."

"But, Mami . . ."

"Felita, we just moved here. We are not going to act like them, so that they can say we are as ugly and mean as they are. Besides I'm sure they are just a few troublemakers. They are not everybody in this neighborhood. Let's just go on with our lives, honey." Mami reached over to hug me, but I turned away.

"They started it! I didn't do anything!" At that moment I was so angry at Mami. Didn't she understand what they had done to me?

"Felita, come on. Never you mind them. They are not important in our lives. We have too many things to do to worry about such people. Anyway, look at that!" Mami pointed to my dress. "The hemline is turned up. You are lucky this day. Do you know what that means?"

"No." I shook my head.

"Well, when that happens the very first time a person wears a dress, there's a true saying. It's a custom I heard, that if that person kisses the upturned hemline and wishes for a new dress, she'll get one!"

"Really?" Quickly I kissed the upturned hemline, closed my eyes, and wished for my yellow party dress.

The very next evening there on my bed was the most beautiful bright-yellow party dress. Sparkling like the sun, with a lace collar and velvet trimming, almost exactly like Gigi's. Mami was right. My wish had come true! Now I could wear the dress to Gigi's party next week.

Mami gave me permission to stay overnight after Gigi's party. I got there early and helped set things up. Everybody said Gigi and I looked just like sisters. We had even combed our hair in exactly the same way. It was so good to be back where everybody was friendly and to see my friends again. When anyone asked me how I liked my new neighborhood, I just answered that I would rather be living back here. I didn't mention what had happened to me. All I wanted to do right now was just forget about those mean girls.

We had such a great time at that party. There were door prizes for everybody and lots of games to play. We played musical chairs. I almost won that game. We bobbed for apples in the bathtub. Some of the kids got soaking wet. The best part was when Gigi's cousin, Eduardo, performed magic tricks for us. Eduardo goes to college and does magic for parties, birthdays, all kinds of occasions. Mrs. Mercado, Gigi's mother, says that's how he makes extra money for himself. He calls himself Eduardo the Magic Maker. He was so good. He cracked jokes, did card tricks, and made coins and even a large pitcher of milk disappear. We put on lots of good records and danced. It was all fabulous.

After the party, Gigi and I helped the grown-ups

clean up. Then we got ready for bed. Most of the time I share just about everything with Gigi, but somehow I couldn't bring myself to talk about those nasty girls and the way they had ganged up on me. I knew that what Mami had said to me was right. Anyway I couldn't have fought back, not alone—there had been too many of them. Also the grown-ups had scared me too. Still I wanted to do something . . . punch a couple of them, make them cry just like they had done to me. I hated to go back to that awful neighborhood, but that's where we lived now, and I knew I had no choice.

Gigi and I talked long into the night. We spoke about all kinds of things but not about what was really bothering me.

At my new home I stayed indoors most of the time. Mami didn't urge me to go outside. Nobody in our family said much about what had happened. At first my brothers were very angry and wanted to find out who had hit me, but my parents said it was best to forget about it.

"These are just some troublemakers. I'm sure it won't happen a second time. People have to get used to us, that's all," Papi had said. "But once they see we are just like anybody else, we will settle in and be just plain neighbors."

When I did have to pass by any of those mean girls on the street, I just made believe I didn't see them. They also ignored me. For about another week or so things stayed this way. Then late one afternoon Mami and I were getting supper ready when we heard someone pounding on our door and screaming. Mami hurried to open the door and there was Johnny, sobbing like a baby. I had never seen Johnny cry like that. He was all doubled over holding his sides. His library books were strewn about on the floor. Mami let out a scream.

"Johnny, Johnny! Qué pasa? What's wrong?" Johnny lifted his head. His nose was bleeding and there was a cut on his lower lip, which was swollen. "Are you all right, muchacho?" Mami went on trying to talk to him, asking questions. Johnny kept moaning and crying. "Come in the house, son. Oh, my God . . . por Dios!" The door of one of the apartments opposite ours opened for an instant, then slammed shut. "Felita, pick up his books and papers. Go on, hurry up!" She took Johnny inside.

As I began to pick up his books the door right next
to ours opened very slowly. Mrs. Halahan, the old
lady who lives there, poked out her head.

"Tsk, tsk, what happened?" she asked in a whisper.

"I don't know. But my brother Johnny is hurt."

"You know, you are nice people, I can see that. But
you don't belong here . . . that's all there is to it!
You people should know this, for your own good."
Quickly she shut her door, and I heard her bolt the
lock.

My mother's face looked frightened and worried.
I could see she was trying hard not to cry. Gently she
washed Johnny's face with a warm washcloth. They
were in the kitchen. Johnny was seated, and Mami
was standing over him.

"There, that's not so bad. I think it looks worse
than it is."

"What happened?" I asked.

"They beat me up, that's what!" Johnny said.

"Who, Johnny?"

"Some hoodlums, that's who," Mami answered.
"And we are going to find out who they are. Wait
till your father hears about this."

"A gang of big guys, around fifteen and sixteen
years old, walked up to me when I was coming into

our building," Johnny said. "They asked me where I thought I was going. I said, 'In there, where I live.' 'You don't live there,' the biggest guy told me. I think he's their leader or something. I said, 'Yes, I live on the third floor, apartment 34-B.' 'Not anymore you don't, *spick*!' he said, and they all began to shove me around. When I told them to leave me alone, they all began to hit me. I hit them back, and then they punched and kicked me. I blocked them as much as I could until I got a chance to run inside the building. Once I ran up the stairs, they took off."

"There was nobody around to help you, Johnny?" Mami asked. Johnny shook his head. "They see a young boy like this being abused and they don't do nothing. It's inhuman!"

"They don't want us here. They hate us!" Johnny screamed. "They're always calling Tito and me names. Look what they done to Felita. I hate them too! I wanna get out of here. Why did we ever have to move to this rotten place anyway?"

Mami turned to look at me. I could see the tears beginning to fill her eyes. She swallowed and composed herself a little. "Never mind all that now. Wait till Papi gets home. We'll figure this out, you'll see."

"Sure!" Johnny looked at Mami, then at me. "I'll

bet!" Quickly he left the kitchen, and we could hear him slam the door of his bedroom.

"Felita," Mami said, "we are going to work this out."

All I could do was shrug my shoulders and leave just like Johnny. I didn't much believe Mami either.

That evening my parents went to complain to the super. They wanted to know who had attacked Johnny. When they returned, we asked what had happened.

"Nobody around here knows nothing," Papi said. "The super told us the landlord wants to see us. Okay, I want to see him too. Maybe he can tell me what's going on around here!"

"Man, I'd like to find those suckers that hurt my brother," Tito said. "Then I'd go back to our old block and get me a hold of some bad dudes. Some of them guys owe me a favor. We would come back here and bust backsides, beat them so bad . . ."

"Hold on!" Papi interrupted. "Right away you're gonna start beating up people too, eh? Big shot here! You just calm down. Nobody is gonna beat up anybody. You hear? You don't go making plans to get anybody for anything!" Tito glared at Papi. "Hey, did you hear me? Answer!"

"Yeah." Tito sat sulking.

"I don't know what's going on here," Mami said. "Alberto, we move to a better neighborhood and our kids get beat up. It's worse than where we used to live."

"That's right," Johnny said. "We don't like it here. Let's move back."

"I hate it here," I said. "I wanna go too."

"You see, Rosa? What you started?" Papi was shouting. "We just moved here. How we gonna move back? By magic? Now all of you calm down!"

"You are the one shouting!" Mami said.

"All right." Papi stopped and looked at all of us. "Let's not fight among ourselves, eh? We don't need this. Look, let's give it a try here. These people are bullies. We shouldn't let them know we are afraid. Now I'm going to speak to Mr. Geller, the landlord. When we rented from him, he knew we were Puerto Rican. Nobody lied to him. We have a right to live in peace in our home and in our neighborhood."

"This ain't my neighborhood!" Tito whispered.

"Tito, cut it out!" Papi said. "You are going to help in this. We don't need another troublemaker. Besides" —Papi smiled—"you wanna beat somebody up, try me." He went over to Tito playfully and began to box around him and jab him gently. Tito stood up and began to jab Papi back. We all watched as they danced around each other trying to land punches. Naturally Papi got the best of Tito. He always does. And then he lets Tito land a blow and makes believe Tito knocked him out. Finally Papi gets up and picks up Tito's arm declaring him the champ. We've all seen this before, but every time they go through the routine it's funny.

"The champ, the one and only," Papi announced, "Tito Maldonado." Everybody laughed. "Okay, now we pull together as a family. We don't fight each other."

Mr. Geller, the landlord, told my parents that he thought it would be best for everybody if we moved out. He even said that our deposit of a month's extra rent could be used for next month as long as we left as soon as possible.

Still my parents felt we should stay.

"We have plans for our family, same as everybody else." Papi had answered. "We made sacrifices to move here and pay this rent. Nobody is gonna put us out so easily."

Another week and a half went by. No one said hello to us or gave us a friendly greeting. Our smiles were ignored. I never went out to play. Mami insisted that none of us kids be outside by ourselves. My brothers had to come and go together. If they were a little bit late, Mami would worry. We kept to ourselves, mostly confined to our apartment. But we began to feel that perhaps the trouble had stopped, and no one was out to harm us.

Then, one morning, Johnny went down to get the mail and found our mailbox lock broken. Our mail was opened and scattered all over the floor. None of the other mailboxes had been damaged in any way.

"How could they?" Papi was furious. "Tampering with the mail is a federal offense. They could go to jail for that!"

"And who do we complain to?" Mami asked. "The super is going to say it was just kids having a little 'fun.' The landlord is going to tell us to move out. If we go to the police, they will take our names and look into it. When they come around to investigate, God knows what these people will tell the police about us. Alberto, next time I worry they will break down our door and hurt us in our own home. It's only gonna get worse, not better. I can't take this any longer. Let's leave."

"Enough. Rosa, for pity's sakes! You know what it

took for us to move here! How many hours of my
working overtime, and you scrimping and saving, eh?
I'm going down to talk to that superintendent. There
must be someone in this place we can talk to!" Papi
rushed out in a rage.

I looked at my brothers and they looked at me.
Without saying a word we all knew how each one of
us felt. We wanted to leave here and the sooner the
better.

When Papi returned, Mami asked what had happened.

" 'Just a couple of kids playing pranks on grown-
ups.' Can you imagine?" Papi shook his head. "I can't
believe he said that!"

"What are we going to do, Alberto?" Mami asked.

"Rosa, if there is one more thing done against us,
we'll get out. I promise. But let's give it another
chance here. It's a big step now for us to move again.
Let's see how things go for a while."

Then, one afternoon, Mami was returning from the
supermarket lugging her heavy shopping cart. As she
approached our building she noticed that everyone
who had been on the stoop swiftly disappeared. Mami
began to climb the stoop steps, pulling her shopping
cart up behind her. All of a sudden there was an ex-

plosion of water and a loud crash. A paper sack filled with water had been thrown from above and smashed right on Mami's shopping cart. Then a second sack exploded against the stone steps, showering her feet with cold water. Mami looked at the windows above but saw no one. She looked out at an empty street.

When she got upstairs, Mami was shaking. She told us what had happened to her.

"I cannot take this any longer," she said. "I'm going to speak to your father. Alberto must know we can't stay here."

"I'd like to kill them!" said Tito.

All I knew was that I wanted to get away from all these people who hated us. I didn't know why they hated us or what we had done, except that we were Puerto Rican. Somehow that made them very angry.

"A sack full of water coming down with such a force could have hurt me badly. I could have gotten a concussion! First it was Felita, then Johnny, now me. I'm scared! I'm afraid to let my children walk out of this apartment and into that street. Okay, they don't have to like us, but to hate so much that they use violence? No, it's too much!" Mami was still very upset that evening when she spoke to Papi.

"Rosa, you are right. Either they will harm us or I

will end up by hurting someone badly. It's time to leave. Bueno, we'll get out!"

My parents were sad, but my brothers and I were overjoyed. We all hoped and prayed we could move back to our old block. I couldn't wait to look around the cheaperia store again and buy some of that delicious dulce de coco at Doña Josefina's bodega. But best of all I could play outdoors again, share things with Gigi, and just hang out with my good friends. I couldn't wait to get away from that awful street and those mean people who, no matter what we did or didn't do, were always there ready to hurt us.

• three •

Abuelita

It took a few weeks, but by the middle of August my parents found an apartment in a building right on our old block.

"We're fortunate that some of our good friends helped us find this place," Papi said.

Our new building was across the street from where we used to live. This apartment was smaller than the one we had just left. Mami and Papi had the big bedroom, my brothers shared the other bedroom, but I didn't have a real room. It was more like a kind of hallway storage area between the kitchen and living room. There was no door, but Mami had put up curtains at both entrances for privacy. There was just enough space for my bed, a chest of drawers, and a stool. And even though we hadn't lived in that new place for very long, Mami said she missed her nice large kitchen.

None of that bothered me very much. It was just great to be back. At first I noticed that our old neighborhood wasn't as clean as the one we had just come from and that here it was a lot noisier and more crowded. But seeing my friends and feeling so welcome more than made up for that prettier looking street. When some of the neighbors or kids asked me how come we moved back so fast, I simply said that we didn't like it where we were, that we would all rather live right here with our friends, which after all was true. Still these questions were kind of upsetting. They reminded me of those awful girls and what they had done to me.

Abuelita, my grandmother, was giving us a welcome-back dinner. I love to eat at my abuelita's. She is the most wonderful cook in the whole world. Her flan—

egg custard—is fantastic to eat! It is even better than Mami's, although I would never say such a thing out loud.

Abuelita is my father's mother. She lives with her brother, Tío Jorge. Although Abuelita came here as a widow from Puerto Rico many, many years ago, she still only speaks Spanish. Papi says that Tío Jorge learned to speak English right away, but not Abuelita. She is very old, older than Tío Jorge. She has real white hair that gleams like the snow when moonlight shines on it. Her face has many, many lines. When she smiles, and she smiles a whole lot, all the lines move around and change. I love her so much. When I am a pest, una molestosa, as Mami calls me, Abuelita doesn't lose her patience. All the others yell at me. But not her. She always talks to me gently or gives me a treat.

After we all finished eating dinner and everyone got ready to leave, I asked Abuelita if I could stay overnight.

"My goodness, qué bueno!" she said with a smile. "It's been such a long time since you asked to stay with me. This is a real treat. Let me ask Rosa. If she gives you permission, you may stay with me."

I was glad Mami said I could stay. Actually I wanted to talk to Abuelita about what had happened to me with those girls.

I liked Abuelita's small apartment. She had two songbirds and a parakeet. They lived in little bright-colored bird cages. There were lots of plants all around the house. Abuelita had one small shelf altar in her bedroom. There a lighted candle always burned, set into a small red glass holder in front of a framed holy picture. She had told me that it was a picture of Saint Francis of Assisi, patron saint of animals. He was Abuelita's favorite saint.

After everyone left, Abuelita gave me some more of her delicious flan. Then we made up the daybed in the living room and got ready for bed.

"Felita," Tío Jorge said, "before you go back home, I have some nature cards to show you. They list all the different birds that live in the northeastern region of the United States and the kinds of trees and plants that grow there as well."

"Great," I said. I loved to look at Tío Jorge's books and collection of nature cards. He had a great collection, because he loved animals and nature.

"Tomorrow, then, yes?"

"Yes," I said.

After Tío Jorge went to his room, Abuelita took me to her big bed for a while. We snuggled up real close, nice and warm. This was always my favorite time when I stayed overnight.

"Now, mi Felita. Do you want to hear a story?" she asked.

"Not tonight, Abuelita."

"No?" She really sounded surprised. "This is the first time I ever heard you say no to a story. You must have something very important on your mind."

"How did you know?"

"Oh, I know. I can tell."

"How, Abuelita?"

"Well, when you get to be as old as me, and you love someone as much as I care for you, then you don't need words. You know what the other person feels."

"Really?"

"Oh, yes, that's a fact." We were both silent for a minute. "Now whatever is troubling your mind like this must come out. Tell me, Felita."

"Abuelita, I don't want Mami or anybody else to know that I . . . I feel like this."

"Like how, Felita?"

"Bad . . . and like I can't stand up for myself."

"Well, then, I promise you, nobody will know but us, yes?" She smiled and hugged me real tight.

"It's about when I lived in that new neighborhood and what happened to me." I told Abuelita the whole story, just like it happened. "Probably Mami told you already, but I don't think she really knows how I feel."

"Now what makes you say that?"

"Abuelita, I never said anything to those girls. Never. It was as if they were right, because I just walked away, you know? I wish I could go back and beat them all up! And also tell them off—tell them a whole lot of nasty things about them and their families. I would like to hurt them, just like they hurt me."

"Felita, you will always meet some mean people and bullies in this world. What your mother told you was right. You must feel strength here"—Abuelita put her hand over her heart—"inside. You were brave, Felita. You must know that, yes?" She paused, then went on. "What I said and what Rosa said is not enough, eh? You are not satisfied, right?" I nodded. "All right, then, let's figure this out. I don't think that hurting them is going to make anything better or really count right now. After all, what happened is over. You are far away from there. But, maybe you could be prepared for the future. When you come across people like this, you could let them know how ignorant they are. Yes?"

"Yes, Abuelita."

"When anybody in the future gives you a hard time about the way your family looks, let them know that Puerto Ricans are part of all the different races on this earth. We Puerto Ricans are a rainbow of earth colors! Just like the many flowers of one garden. And that garden is the island of Puerto Rico. Although sometimes we grow pretty flowers right here, just like you!" Abuelita paused and I laughed, pleased. "Don't be afraid to open up your mouth and let them know, eh?"

"Okay, Abuelita."

"And when these ignoramuses criticize or correct you because you use Spanish words, let them know how much better off you are. Look how you and I can speak in Spanish together. This already makes you twice as smart as people who only speak one language. Finally, when anyone says, 'Go back to where you came from' or 'You don't belong here,' tell them Puerto Ricans, whether they're born on the island of Puerto Rico or here in the mainland United States, are American citizens. But the most important thing is for you to remember that everyone can feel sorrow or be hurt by others. We all share the same basic feelings and wants." Abuelita paused and winked at me. "My goodness, even the rich and powerful use the bathroom, just like you and me." We both laughed loudly. "Even the Queen of England too . . ."

"Abuelita"—I giggled—"even Mr. Johnson, the vice-principal?"

"Even him." We both laughed some more. Abuelita was silent for a little while. "Felita, it is important for you to know that no one is better than anyone else because they have a lighter skin or a different kind of hair. Inside you must know this and feel strong. Do you understand, Felita?"

"Yes, Abuelita."

"Sometimes when people gang up on you and you are alone, there is not much to be done. Except what you did, Felita. You did the right thing. But having that strength in you will help. That is what your mother was trying to tell you. Understand?"

"I understand, Abuelita."

"Now it's time for us to get some sleep. I'm tired. How about you?"

"I want to ask you one more thing, Abuelita."

"All right," she said, sighing, "but only one more thing."

"Remember how you always told me stories of Puerto Rico? And you said we could visit one day? When do you think we can go?"

"I hope we can go before I leave this earth, Felita. When exactly, I cannot say. But it would make me happy to go back. I haven't been to Puerto Rico for so many years."

"Please, just tell me a little bit about Puerto Rico and where you lived again. Please!"

"Okay." Abuelita got up. "But first you go to your daybed, and I'll tuck you in. Then I'll tell you."

I lay down. Abuelita covered me and sat beside me.

"You know all about the wonderful gardens in Puerto Rico, don't you?" I nodded. "And about the brightest red flowers that grow on beautiful trees?"

"They are flamboyan trees. Right, Abuelita?"

"Right. Well, where I used to live there were lots of wild flowers that always surprised and delighted anyone who passed by. Why, you never saw so many marvelous colors. I used to love to pick them. There you can pick flowers, not like here, where they give you a fine if you touch the flowers. Well, anyway, I would make the most beautiful bouquets."

Abuelita's voice was so soothing that without even knowing when, I fell fast asleep.

· four ·

A Hot Summer Night

It was still summer, almost the end of August. The best part of summer was that we were all able to stay up late into the night. On real hot evenings we opened the fire hydrant, and the police would attach a sprinkler to the large round spout. All of us would jump right into the spray of cool water and get soaking wet. It was so much fun just to hang out on the block and play with my friends.

The grown-ups sat in front of their buildings, mostly

on folding chairs. They talked and greeted people passing by while still keeping an eye on us. Mami usually took her mending to work on. Some of the other women took all different kinds of needlework. They always complained that the streetlights were not bright enough and their eyes hurt from the strain of working in semidarkness. Some of the men set up card tables and played dominoes. Often Papi and the other men listened to the ball game on his transistor radio. They made small bets with one another about which team would win or which player would score most. When they got excited, they began to argue loudly and yell. The women would tell them to calm down and stop the noise. There would be a lot of discussion and laughing before the men calmed down. This went on just about every evening.

I always watched for the piragua man and his cart. The piragua man had a scraper at the end of a metal scooper. He would scrape real hard on a large block of ice. Then he emptied the crushed ice into a paper cone and asked you to pick your favorite syrup. There were all different kinds of flavors: strawberry, cherry, peppermint, pineapple, and lots more. My favorite was cherry. He would soak the ice with lots of syrup. Piraguas were called snowballs in English. I could always count on at least one grown-up to give me enough money to buy a piragua. Once in a while I even got money for ice cream or Doña Josefina's coconut candy.

We played nonstop until we got too tired to go on. By that time the shops on our block began to close. Doña Josefina would be the first to close her bodega. Old Bernie's candy store would be last. When Old Bernie's lights went out, it was like a signal for everyone to head home.

Getting up the next day was no problem because Mami let me sleep right into late morning.

One summer night as we were all getting ready for bed we heard screaming and yelling. Usually by this time our street was quiet and empty. The noise startled us all. We ran into the living room and looked down into the street.

"Fire!"

"Fire. Fuego! Fuego . . . help!"

The shouting sounded right up into our apartment. We saw several people rushing around.

"Look! Mira, mira!" A man pointed over to Old Bernie's candy store. Thick black clouds of smoke were gushing out of it.

"We must call the firemen right away!" Mami said.

"Has anybody called the fire department?" Papi shouted down to the people in the street.

"Yes, we have. Come down and help!" they yelled.

"Right away." Papi was already dressed and on his way out.

"Poor old Bernie," Mami said. "I hope he's all right."

Old Bernie lived in the back of his candy store with his cat, Mr. Roosevelt.

"Come on, kids, let's get dressed." Mami rushed to get our clothes. "Here, everybody, let's go. This fire is very close to our building. I think we should be out in the street, just in case."

"Just in case? What do you mean, Mami?" My heart seemed to leap and skip around my insides.

"Sometimes these fires can swallow up a whole block in minutes. These old tenements catch fire just like dry timber. We are only two buildings away from Old Bernie's store."

"Are we gonna have a fire *here too*?" I screamed. All of a sudden everybody was rushing around me.

"Everybody. Johnny, Tito, calm down. Felita, don't be silly." Mami put her arm around me. "Let's all keep our heads now. I'm only making extra sure nothing happens to us, that's all. No need for anyone to be frightened. I want everybody to get their clothes on. Hurry and keep calm."

In spite of the fact that I still felt scared, I managed to get dressed fast. We were all ready and out in the hallway in minutes. Some of our neighbors were still in nightclothes, rushing about, asking questions.

"All right," Mami said, "Tito, you take your sister outside. On your way down knock hard on every door that's closed. Yell 'Fire on our block.' I'm going to knock on doors on the upper floors."

Several neighbors joined us as we ran knocking on doors and shouting for everyone's safety. As soon as we got outside, we heard the screaming sirens of the fire engines. The bright-red trucks with their flashing lights filled our street. The beams of light bounced from building to building and the smell of the fire was stifling. The air was thick with smoke. It looked like a gray fog. My eyes burned and my throat felt scratchy. Now there were flames coming out of Old Bernie's candy store. Upstairs in the building above the fire several people looked out their windows.

"Get out of the building!" people in the street shouted up at them. "Go up on the roof—get out!"

"Are they gonna jump out the windows?" I asked Tito. I was afraid to look up.

"No," he said. "The firemen will put up ladders to get them out. Don't worry."

Johnny came over to us. "Come on, Felita, stay with me," he said. "It's gonna be all right." Johnny held me close to him and I felt better.

There was a loudspeaker on one of the trucks. A voice blared out instructions to the firemen, who rushed about trying to work as fast as possible. Quickly they cleared a large area of the street and attached long hoses to the fire hydrants. Immediately jets of water doused the fire. Ladders were being set up to get to the people on the upper floors. Several firemen carrying axes, crowbars, and hoses rushed into the hallway of the building. We heard glass, wood, and concrete smashing as the firemen fought their way into Old Bernie's candy store.

I had never seen a fire this close up before. The firemen worked so swiftly. They did not seem afraid of the flames, intense heat, or smoke.

"We tried to get into the store, but there was too much smoke and fire," Papi said. "I think the people upstairs will be okay, though. The firemen got here just in time."

"I hope Old Bernie's all right." Mami shook her

head. "Poor fellow. What a pity, bendito. He's all alone in there."

"Except for Mr. Roosevelt," I reminded Mami.

I had asked Old Bernie once why he called his cat Mr. Roosevelt. He told me that his cat was named after a great president of the United States, Franklin Delano Roosevelt. This was an honor, Old Bernie said, because he loved his cat even more than this president.

All the flames were out by now, though the smoke was still dense. I heard the firemen say that they didn't need the ladders. The people on the upper floors were safe now.

"The fire only went up as far as the first landing," said Mami.

"Yes, but I wonder how my apartment is. I hope nothing is damaged." Mrs. Lopez began to cry. "My apartment is right over the candy store."

"Never mind," Mr. Lopez said. "We got our lives, and that's worth more than anything."

"I wonder how that fire got started," someone said.

"I wish I knew myself," Mrs. Lopez replied. "I know it started in the candy store."

"Have they found Bernie?" someone asked.

"Where is he?" someone else cried out.

"Poor man," Mr. Lopez said. "I hope he's okay."

"Do you think Old Bernie's all burned up?" I asked Johnny.

"I don't know," he said. "I hope not."

What if he's all burned up and dead? I asked myself. And Mr. Roosevelt too? I looked around me at all the confusion. I wanted to go home right away. I didn't want to be there when they found Old Bernie and Mr. Roosevelt all burned and looking like who knows what. The whole thing gave me the shivers.

"Johnny, I wanna go home."

"We can't yet. We gotta wait and see what happens and what Papi and Mami have to say. They went over to try to talk to the firemen."

"I don't wanna wait. I want to leave now."

"Well, you can't! So just be still and wait like everybody else," he said firmly.

I thought of walking away and going on upstairs to my room, but my block looked so different with the firetrucks and all the people standing around. Everybody seemed to be talking at once, shouting above the noise coming from the firetrucks. I felt safer right here, next to Johnny, and decided to stay put. If they did find Old Bernie and Mr. Roosevelt . . . looking awful . . . I would just shut my eyes real tight.

All of a sudden we saw two firemen with oxygen tanks strapped to their backs coming out of the building. They were helping someone who was wrapped up in a blanket.

"Who is it?"

"Who've they got there?"

Everyone was asking lots of questions. I watched as they helped the person out into the street. My stomach felt queasy. Oh, here it comes! I shut my eyes tightly.

"Look," shouted Johnny. "It's him!"

I opened my eyes and looked. Sure enough, it was Old Bernie, alive!

"It's Old Bernie!" a neighbor shouted. There was a loud cheer. And he smiled happily to everyone. Then he held up something that was wrapped in a towel. He removed the towel and showed everyone . . . Mr. Roosevelt. There was an even louder cheer from the crowd.

"Hurray for Old Bernie and Mr. Roosevelt!"

"Hallelujah, praise the Lord!" Mrs. Hairston shouted. She was the minister of the Baptist storefront church by the corner.

Everyone was really happy that Old Bernie and Mr. Roosevelt were still alive.

There was still a lot of commotion near the candy store. The firemen and policemen were talking to the tenants of the building. People were milling about and trying to get a look inside the burned store. There were broken glass and bricks all over the sidewalk.

An ambulance came and took Old Bernie away.

"Is he gonna stay in the hospital?" I asked Johnny.

"No, he's just going to get checked out, that's all. He'll be okay."

The candy store was closed and boarded up now. Everyone began to leave. Finally Papi told us all to get upstairs. I got into bed but it was quite some time before I could think of sleep. It had really been a scary sight, all that smoke and flames. The worst thing had been thinking poor Old Bernie and his cat might be dead. Boy, was I glad when I saw him and Mr. Roosevelt alive and looking like they always did. I wondered if he would be able to open his candy store again. It looked like a great big mess to me. I heard Mami's voice. She was in the kitchen talking to Papi.

"I tell you, Alberto, I wish we could move away from here. Even though our street is not one of the worst ones in this neighborhood, these buildings were old half a century ago. Now they're decrepit fire traps."

"Well, we can't. We can't go nowhere right now," Papi answered. "The last move we made cost us everything we had and then some. Besides, even though this neighborhood is supposed to be more dangerous than the other one—more muggings, gangs of tough kids—we had to be afraid for our very lives over there. Where are we gonna start running to now? And with what? Let's just do the best we can here. Let's be careful."

"And lucky," Mami said. "Alberto, I just hope it'll be all right for the kids back here."

"It's up to us, Rosa. We gotta make it good. We just gotta work harder and make sure we keep an eye on them. Keep them doing right, that's all. Bad influences take over only when kids are not looked after."

"Oh, I suppose you are right. We'll manage." I heard Mami give a big sigh. "Tomorrow we'll see what can be done for those who lost things in the fire."

"We'll do the best we can, Rosa." Papi paused. "I wonder how that fire got started? So far no one seems to know. But of course Bernie is an old man. He's all alone in there. Could have been some oversight on his part. Maybe that store is too much for him."

"I don't know," said Mami, sounding worried. "Poor Bernie, that candy store and his cat are all he has."

"Let's go to bed now," Papi said. "That's enough for one night. I got to get to work early tomorrow."

I hoped we weren't going to move again. Even if we did have that awful fire, I loved my block and my friends. After a while I got used to the burning smell still in the air and shut my eyes.

Mami said that what had saved Old Bernie in the fire was that he had wrapped himself up in a wet blanket. Then he wrapped up Mr. Roosevelt in a wet towel. He had escaped by climbing out the back window and into the alleyway. There he had waited for the firemen to come and get him. Everybody said it was a miracle that nobody had been seriously hurt in the fire.

Soon afterward Old Bernie had to retire. Mami and Papi said that he couldn't recover his losses. He went to live with his sister and her husband far away, upstate, in the country. He took Mr. Roosevelt with him.

The neighborhood did not seem the same without Old Bernie and Mr. Roosevelt. Everybody missed them a lot.

The new owners of the candy store were not nearly as nice as Old Bernie. They didn't even call their store a candy store. It had a brand-new sign that read: THE ALVAREZ TOBACCO AND STATIONERY SHOP. A lot of damage had been caused by the fire. The whole store had been renovated. The old wooden ice cream and soda counter with the separate sections for different flavors of ice cream and syrup was gone. And the shelf that held the wooden drawers filled with loose candy was also gone.

This new store only had a small counter with space for candy, gum, cigarettes, and all kinds of tobacco. Mr. and Mrs. Alvarez sold mostly magazines, comic books, newspapers, greeting cards, and stationery. Some packaged ice cream was for sale. They didn't like anyone to hang out in their store. They watched us all the time. They were always rushing us out, making comments, like "What do you want? Let's go, kids! Come on, hurry up. What's taking you brats so long? *Outside!*" and so on.

Like it or not, they were the new owners, and that was the only candy store on our block. We learned not to pay too much attention to them, and always to go in as a group. This way, they couldn't really pick on any one kid. After a while, we all began to get used to them.

Still, we all wondered what had caused the fire in the first place. Some people were afraid it was arson. That was because just two weeks before, some big teen-agers had been caught trying to set fire to a warehouse not too far from our block. But no one really knew how the fire had started.

For a long time afterward Mami was very nervous about making sure the stove and oven were turned off. And she was always saying she smelled smoke, even though there wasn't any smoke to smell.

· five ·

Thanksgiving

A wonderful thing happened this new school year. Gigi, Consuela, Paquito, and I were all going into the fourth grade, and we were put in the same class. It had never happened before. Once I was in the same class with Consuela, and last year Gigi and Paquito were together. But this—it was too good to be true! Of course knowing Gigi and I were in the same class made me the happiest.

Our teacher, Miss Lovett, was friendly and laughed

easily. In early October, after we had all settled into our class and gotten used to the routine of school once more, Miss Lovett told us that this year our class was going to put on a play for Thanksgiving. The play we were going to perform was based on a poem by Henry Wadsworth Longfellow, called "The Courtship of Miles Standish." It was about the Pilgrims and how they lived when they first landed in America.

We were all so excited about the play. Miss Lovett called for volunteers to help with the sets and costumes. Paquito and I agreed to help with the sets. Consuela was going to work on makeup. Gigi had not volunteered for anything. When we asked her what she was going to do, she shrugged and didn't answer.

Miss Lovett said we could all audition for the different parts in the play. I was really interested in being Priscilla. She is the heroine. Both Captain Miles Standish and the handsome, young John Alden are in love with her. She is the most beautiful maiden in Plymouth, Massachusetts. That's where the Pilgrims used to live. I told my friends how much I would like to play that part. Everyone said I would be perfect . . . except Gigi. She said that it was a hard part to do, and maybe I wouldn't be able to play it. I really got annoyed and asked her what she meant.

"I just don't think you are right to play Priscilla. That's all," she said.

"What do you mean by right?" I asked. But Gigi only shrugged and didn't say another word. She was beginning to get on my nerves.

Auditions for the parts were going to start Tuesday. Lots of kids had volunteered to audition. Paquito said he would try out for the brave Captain Miles Standish. Consuela said she was too afraid to get up in front of everybody and make a fool of herself. Gigi didn't show any interest in the play and refused to even talk to us about it. Finally the day came for the girls to read for the part of Priscilla. I was so excited I could hardly wait. Miss Lovett had given us some lines to study. I had practiced real hard. She called out all the names of those who were going to read. I was surprised when I heard her call out "Georgina Mercado." I didn't even know Gigi wanted to try out for Priscilla. I looked at Gigi, but she ignored me. We began reading. It was my turn. I was very nervous and kept forgetting my lines. I had to look down at the script a whole lot. Several other girls were almost as nervous as I was. Then it was Gigi's turn. She recited the part almost by heart. She hardly looked at the script. I noticed that she was wearing one of her best dresses.

She had never looked that good in school before. When she finished, everybody clapped. It was obvious that she was the best one. Miss Lovett made a fuss.

"You were just wonderful, Georgina," she said, "made for the part!" Boy, would I have liked another chance. I bet I could have done better than Gigi.

Why hadn't she told me she wanted the part? It's a free country, after all. She could read for the same part as me. I wasn't going to stop her! I was really angry at Gigi.

After school everyone was still making a fuss over her. Even Paquito had to open his stupid mouth.

"Oh, man, Gigi!" he said. "You were really good. I liked the part when John Alden asked you to marry Captain Miles Standish and you said, 'Why don't you speak for yourself, John?' You turned your head like this." Paquito imitated Gigi and closed his eyes. "That was really neat!" Consuela and the others laughed and agreed.

I decided I wasn't walking home with them.

"I have to meet my brothers down by the next street," I said. "I'm splitting. See you." They hardly noticed. Only Consuela said goodbye. The rest just kept on hanging all over Gigi. Big deal, I thought.

Of course walking by myself and watching out for

the tough kids was not something I looked forward to. Just last Friday Hilda Gonzales had gotten beat up and had her entire allowance stolen. And at the beginning of the term Paquito had been walking home by himself and gotten mugged. A bunch of big bullies had taken his new schoolbag complete with pencil and pen case, then left him with a swollen lip. No, sir, none of us ever walked home from school alone if we could help it. We knew it wasn't a safe thing to do. Those mean kids never bothered us as long as we stuck together. Carefully I looked around to make sure none of the bullies were in sight. Then I put some speed under my feet, took my chances, and headed for home.

Just before all the casting was completed, Miss Lovett offered me a part as one of the Pilgrim women. All I had to do was stand in the background like a zombie. It wasn't even a speaking part.

"I don't get to say one word," I protested.

"Felicidad Maldonado, you are designing the stage sets and you're assistant stage manager. I think that's quite a bit. Besides, all the speaking parts are taken."

"I'm not interested, thank you," I answered.

"You know"—Miss Lovett shook her head—"you can't be the best in everything."

I turned and left. I didn't need to play any part at all. Who cared?

Gigi came over to me the next day with a great big smile all over her face. I just turned away and made believe she wasn't there.

"Felita, are you taking the part of the Pilgrim woman?" she asked me in her sweetest voice, just like nothing had happened.

"No," I said, still not looking at her. If she thought I was going to fall all over her like those dummies, she was wasting her time.

"Oh," was all she said, and walked away. Good, I thought. I don't need her one bit!

At home Mami noticed something was wrong.

"Felita, what's the matter? You aren't going out at all. And I haven't seen Gigi for quite a while. In fact I haven't seen any of your friends."

"Nothing is the matter, Mami. I just got lots of things to do."

"You're not upset because we couldn't give you a birthday party this year, are you?" Mami asked. "You know how hard the money situation has been for us."

My birthday had been at the beginning of November. We had celebrated with a small cake after dinner, but there had been no party.

"No. It's not that," I said and meant it. Even though I had been a little disappointed, I also knew Mami and Papi had done the best they could.

"We'll make it up to you next year, Felita, you'll see."

"I don't care, Mami. It's not important now."

"You didn't go having a fight with Gigi or something? Did you?"

"Now why would I have a fight with anybody!"

"Don't raise your voice, miss," Mami said. "Sorry I asked. But you just calm down."

The play was going to be performed on the day before Thanksgiving. I made the drawings for most of the scenery. I made a barn, a church, trees and grass, cows, and a horse. I helped the others make a real scarecrow. We used a broom and old clothes. Paquito didn't get the part of Captain Miles Standish, but he made a wonderful fence out of cardboard. It looked just like a real wooden fence. Consuela brought in her mother's old leftover makeup. She did a good job of making up everybody.

By the time we set up the stage, everything looked beautiful. Gigi had tried to talk to me a few times. But I just couldn't be nice back to her. She acted like

nothing had happened, like I was supposed to forget she hadn't told me she was going to read for the part! I wasn't going to forget that just because she was now Miss Popularity. She could go and stay with all her newfound friends for all I cared!

The morning of the play, at breakfast, everybody noticed how excited I was.

"Felita," Papi exclaimed, "stop jumping around like a monkey and eat your breakfast."

"She's all excited about the school play today," Mami said.

"That's right. Are you playing a part in the play?" Papi asked.

"No," I replied.

"But she's done most of the sets. Drawing and designing. Isn't that right, Felita?"

"Mami, it was no big deal."

"That's nice," said Papi. "Tell us about it."

"What kind of sets did you do?" Johnny asked.

"I don't know. Look, I don't want to talk about it."

"Boy, are you touchy today," Tito said with a laugh.

"Leave me alone!" I snapped.

"Okay." Mami stood up. "Enough. Felita, are you finished?" I nodded. "Good. Go to school. When you come back, bring home a better mood. Whatever is bothering you, no need to take it out on us." Quickly I left the table.

"Rosa," I heard Papi say, "sometimes you are too hard on her."

"And sometimes you spoil her, Alberto!" Mami snapped. "I'm not raising fresh kids."

I was glad to get out of there. Who needs them, I thought.

The play was a tremendous hit. Everybody looked wonderful and played their parts really well. The stage was brilliant with the color I had used on my drawings. The background of the countryside, the barn, and just about everything stood out clearly. Ernesto Bratter, the stage manager, said I was a good assistant. I was glad to hear that, because a couple of times I'd had to control my temper on account of his ordering me around. But it had all worked out great.

No doubt about it. Gigi was perfect as Priscilla. Even though the kids clapped and cheered for the entire cast, Gigi got more applause than anybody else. She just kept on taking a whole lot of bows.

Afterward Miss Lovett had a party for our class. We had lots of treats. There was even a record player and we all danced. We had a really good time.

Of course Priscilla, alias Gigi, was the big star. She just couldn't get enough attention. But not from me, that was for sure. After the party Gigi spoke to me.

"Your sets were really great. Everybody said the stage looked wonderful."

"Thanks." I looked away.

"Felita, are you mad at me?"

"Why should I be mad at you?"

"Well, I did get the leading part, but . . ."

"Big deal," I said. "I really don't care."

"You don't? But . . . I . . ."

"Look," I said, interrupting her, "I gotta go. I promised my mother I'd get home early. We have to go someplace."

I rushed all the way home. I didn't know why, but I was still furious at Gigi. What was worse was that I was unhappy about having those feelings. Gigi and I had been real close for as far back as I could remember. Not being able to share things with her really bothered me.

six

Making Up

We had a great Thanksgiving. The dinner was just delicious. Abuelita brought her flan. Tío Jorge brought lots of ice cream. He always brings us kids a treat when he visits. Sometimes he even brings each one of us a small gift—a nature book or crayons for me and puzzles or sports magazines for my brothers. He's really very nice to us. One thing about him is that he's sort of quiet and doesn't talk much. Papi says that

Tío Jorge has been like that as far back as he can remember.

Abuelita asked me if I wanted to go home with her that evening. Boy, was I happy to get away from Mami. I just couldn't face another day of her asking me questions about Gigi, my friends, and my whole life. It was getting to be too much!

It felt good to be with Abuelita in her apartment. Abuelita never questioned me about anything really personal unless I wanted to talk about it. She just waited, and when she sensed that I was worried or something, then she would ask me. Not like Mami. I love Mami, but she's always trying to find out every little thing that happens to me. With my abuelita sometimes we just sit and stay quiet, not talk at all. That was nice too. We fixed the daybed for me. And then Tío Jorge, Abuelita, and I had more flan as usual.

"Would you like to go to the park with me this Sunday?" Tío Jorge asked me.

"Yes."

"We can go to the zoo and later we can visit the ducks and swans by the lake."

"Great!" I said.

Whenever Tío Jorge took me to the zoo, he would

tell me stories about how he, Abuelita, and their brothers and sisters had lived and worked as youngsters taking care of farm animals. These were the only times I ever heard him talk a whole lot.

"It's not just playing, you know," he would say. "Taking care of animals is hard work. Back on our farm in Puerto Rico we worked hard, but we had fun too. Every one of us children had our very own favorite pets. I had a pet goat by the name of Pepe. He used to follow me everywhere." No matter how many times he told me the same stories, I always enjoyed hearing them again.

"Well." Tío Jorge got up. "It's a date then on Sunday, yes?"

"Yes, thank you, Tío Jorge."

"Good night," he said and went off to bed.

Abuelita and I sat quietly for a while, then Abuelita spoke.

"You are getting to be a big girl now, Felita. You just turned nine years old. My goodness! But I still hope you will come to bed with your abuelita for a little while, eh?"

I got into bed and snuggled close to Abuelita. I loved her the best, more than anybody. I hadn't been to stay with her since the summer, and somehow this time things felt different. I noticed how tired Abuelita looked. She wasn't moving as fast as she used to. Also I didn't feel so little next to her anymore.

"Tell me, Felita, how have you been? It seems like a long time since we were together like this." She smiled her wonderful smile at me. Her dark, bright eyes looked deeply into mine. I felt her warmth and happiness.

"I'm okay, Abuelita."

"Tell me about your play at school. Rosa tells me you worked on the stage sets. Was the play a success?"

"It was. It was great. The stage looked beautiful. My drawings stood out really well. I never made such big drawings in my life. There was a farm in the country, a barn, and animals. I made it the way it used to be in the olden days of the Pilgrims. You know, how it was when they first came to America."

"I'm so proud of you. Tell me about the play. Did you act in it?"

"No." I paused. "I didn't want to."

"I see. Tell me a little about the story."

I told Abuelita all about it.

"Who played the parts? Any of your friends?"

"Some."

"Who?"

"Well, this boy Charlie Martinez played John Alden. Louie Collins played Captain Miles Standish. You don't know them. Mary Jackson played the part of the narrator. That's the person who tells the story. You really don't know any of them."

I was hoping she wouldn't ask, but she did.

"Who played the part of the girl both men love?"

"Oh, her? Gigi."

"Gigi Mercado, your best friend?" I nodded. "Was she good?"

"Yes, she was. Very good."

"You don't sound too happy about that."

"I don't care." I shrugged.

"But if she is your best friend, I should think you would care."

"I . . . I don't know if she is my friend anymore, Abuelita."

"Why do you say that?"

I couldn't answer. I just felt awful.

"Did she do something? Did you two argue?" I nodded. "Can I ask what happened?"

"Well, it's hard to explain. But what she did wasn't fair."

"Fair about what, Felita?"

I hadn't spoken about it before. Now with Abuelita it was easy to talk about it.

"Well, we all tried out for the different parts. Everybody knew what everybody was trying out for. But Gigi never told anybody she was going to try out for Priscilla. She kept it a great big secret. Even after I told her that I wanted to try for the part, she kept quiet about it. Do you know what she did say? She said I wasn't right for it . . . it was a hard part and all that bunch of baloney. She just wanted the part for herself, so she was mysterious about the whole thing. Like . . . it was . . . I don't know." I stopped for a moment, trying to figure this whole thing out. "After all, I am supposed to be her best friend . . . her very best friend. Why shouldn't she let me know that she wanted to be Priscilla? I wouldn't care. I let her know my plans. I didn't go sneaking around."

"Are you angry because Gigi got the part?"

It was hard for me to answer. I thought about it for a little while. "Abuelita, I don't think so. She was really good in the part."

"Were you as good when you tried out for Priscilla?"

"No." I looked at Abuelita. "I stunk." We both laughed.

"Then maybe you are not angry at Gigi at all."

"What do you mean?"

"Well, maybe you are a little bit . . . hurt?"

"Hurt?" I felt confused.

"Do you know what I think? I think you are hurt because your best friend didn't trust you. From what you tell me, you trusted her, but she didn't have faith in you. What do you think?"

"Yes." I nodded. "Abuelita, yes. I don't know why. Gigi and I always tell each other everything. Why did she act like that to me?"

"Have you asked her?"

"No."

"Why not? Aren't you two speaking to each other?"

"We're speaking. Gigi tried to be friendly a few times."

"Don't you want to stay her friend?"

"I do. Only she came over to me acting like . . . like nothing ever happened. And something did happen! What does she think? That she can go around being sneaky and I'm going to fall all over her? Just because she got the best part, she thinks she's special."

"And you think that's why she came over. Because she wants to be special?"

"I don't know."

"You should give her a chance. Perhaps Gigi acted in a strange way for a reason."

"She wasn't nice to me, Abuelita. She wasn't."

"I'm not saying she was. Or even that she was right. Mira, Felita, friendship is one of the best things in this whole world. It's one of the few things you can't go out and buy. It's like love. You can buy clothes, food, even luxuries, but there's no place I know of where you can buy a real friend. Do you?"

I shook my head. Abuelita smiled at me and waited. We were both silent for a long moment. I wondered if maybe I shouldn't have a talk with Gigi. After all, she had tried to talk to me first.

"Abuelita, do you think it's a good idea for me to . . . maybe talk to Gigi?"

"You know, that's a very good idea." Abuelita nodded.

"Well, she did try to talk to me a few times. Only there's just one thing. I won't know what to say to her. I mean, after what's happened and all."

"After so many years of being close, I am sure you

could say 'Hello, Gigi. How are you?' That should
be easy enough."

"I feel better already, Abuelita."

"Good," Abuelita said. "Now let's you and I get to
sleep. Abuelita is tired."

"You don't have to tuck me in. I'll tuck you in instead." I got out of bed and folded the covers carefully over my side. Then I leaned over her and gave
her a kiss. Abuelita hugged me real tight.

"My Felita has become a young lady," she whispered.

I kept thinking of what Abuelita had said, and on
Monday I waited for Gigi after school. It was as if
she knew I wanted to talk. She came over to me.

"Hello, Gigi," I said. "How are you?"

"Fine." Gigi smiled. "Wanna walk home together?"

"Let's take the long way so we can be by ourselves,"
I said.

We walked without saying anything for a couple
of blocks. Finally I spoke.

"I wanted to tell you, Gigi, you were really great
as Priscilla."

"Did you really like me? Oh, Felita, I'm so glad.

I wanted you to like me, more than anybody else. Of course it was nothing compared to the sets you did. They were something special. Everybody liked them so much."

"You were right too," I said. "I wasn't very good for the part of Priscilla."

"Look." Gigi stopped walking and looked at me. "I'm sorry about . . . about the way I acted. Like, I didn't say anything to you or the others. But, well, I was scared you all would think I was silly or something. I mean, you wanted the part too. So, I figured, better not say nothing."

"I wouldn't have cared, Gigi. Honest."

"Felita . . . it's just that you are so good at a lot of things. Like, you draw just fantastic. You beat everybody at hopscotch and kick-the-can. You know about nature and animals, much more than the rest of us. Everything you do is always better than . . . what I do! I just wanted this part for me. I wanted to be better than you this time. For once I didn't wanna worry about you. Felita, I'm sorry."

I was shocked. I didn't know Gigi felt that way. I didn't feel better than anybody about anything I did. She looked so upset, like she was about to cry any minute. I could see she was miserable and I wanted to comfort her. I had never had this kind of feeling before in my whole life.

"Well, you didn't have to worry. 'Cause I stunk!" We both laughed with relief. "I think I was the worst one!"

"Oh, no, you weren't." Gigi laughed. "Jenny Fuentes was the most awful."

"Worse than me?"

"Much worse. Do you know what she sounded like? She sounded like this. 'Wha . . . wha . . . why don't you . . . speeek for your . . . yourself *Johnnnn?*" Gigi and I burst into laughter.

"And how about that dummy, Louie Collins? I didn't think he read better than Paquito."

"Right," Gigi agreed. "I don't know how he got through the play. He was shaking so much that I was scared the sets would fall right on his head."

It was so much fun, Gigi and I talking about the play and how we felt about everybody and everything. It was just like before, only better.

· seven ·

Wild Flowers

Winter arrived with a heap of cold weather. Once again we all had to fuss with putting on sweaters, scarves, hats, boots, and bundle up until we could hardly move. We did have a few good snowfalls. At first my friends and I enjoyed playing in the freshly fallen snow, but after so many weeks of winter we grew tired of the cold, the snow, and the slush. By the end of March we all waited eagerly for the warm weather and sunshine to come our way.

At last the beginning of spring was in the air. After it rained, especially, I could smell springtime. I don't know why exactly, but all the different odors lingered longer then. For instance I noticed it when I passed Wong's laundry. The smell of freshly washed clothing and starch filled the air in front of their store. When I passed Doña Josefina's bodega, I could smell the fresh vegetables too. Spring made my sense of smell really keen.

I was always happy in the springtime. But this time I heard some bad news. Mami was the one who told us. She got Johnny, Tito, and me all together.

"Abuelita is sick. Very sick. She will have to go to the hospital. I think you should all know this. Your father is worried about her. I want you children to be understanding with your father. If he is a little impatient or nervous, you must not argue with him. Instead I want you all to be a help at this time."

"Is Abuelita going to get an operation?" I asked.

"Yes."

"Will she be all right?" Tito asked.

"I . . . we don't know for sure. Abuelita is very old."

"Tell us what's wrong with her, Mami," said Johnny.

"There are many things wrong, son. A lot of these things are just because she is so old."

"Can we see her before she goes away?" I asked.

"Yes." Mami nodded. "We are all going to visit her this evening after supper. But I don't want any of you to mention what I have told you. And I don't want you, Felita, to complain to her about anything."

"Complain?" I was annoyed. "I don't complain to Abuelita—I talk to her."

"Never mind what you call it. You just act like you don't have a care in the world, you hear?" Boy, sometimes Mami could really be nasty. "Did you hear what I told you, miss?" I nodded. "I didn't hear your answer, Felita."

"Yes," I said.

That evening we all went over to Abuelita's. Tío Jorge was so glad to see us.

"She's resting inside. There is a bed for her in the hospital for the day after tomorrow. Then we'll see."

"How is she, Tío?" Papi asked.

"Your mother is a sick woman, Alberto," Tío Jorge said. He had lived with Abuelita his whole life. Now the thought of a long separation made him very unhappy.

We all gathered around Abuelita's bedside. She

kissed each of us and asked lots of questions. She looked very skinny and little. But she still smiled a whole lot.

"I tell you," Abuelita said, "I can't get over how the boys have grown. And look at Felita! Every time I see her she is more of a young lady."

After a while Mami told us kids to leave. We sat in the kitchen eating. Tío Jorge had put out some cake and milk for us.

The grown-ups stayed talking with Abuelita for a long time. I had fun watching the little birds in their cages. They were so sweet.

"Abuelita has always had birds," said Johnny, "for as long as I can remember."

"That's right," I agreed.

"Are they the same birds she always had?" asked Tito.

"No. I don't think so," Johnny answered. "I remember different ones when I was very little. Except for the parakeet. She's had him the longest."

"That's true," I said. "She calls him Pepito, after another one that died many years ago. Do you know that framed holy picture Abuelita has in her bedroom?"

"Yeah? What about it?" asked Tito.

"Do you know who he is?"

"I think so. Let me see." Tito thought a while. "I forget, I think it might be—"

"You don't know," I interrupted. "It's St. Francis of Assisi. He's the patron saint of animals. Abuelita told me all about it."

"We knew it, didn't we, Johnny?" Johnny smiled.

"You did not. I had to tell you."

"We did too. Big deal. Right away you have to be a smart aleck."

"Better to be a smart aleck than a stupid aleck!"

"Don't get too smart, Felita," Tito said.

"Okay," Johnny scolded. "Now you two cut it out. Abuelita is sick. This is no time to be arguing."

"She started it, Johnny," Tito protested.

"Cut it out! You're older than her, you should know better." Johnny turned to me. Just as he was about to say something the grown-ups came into the kitchen.

"Abuelita wants to speak to each of you," Papi said. "Johnny, you are the oldest. You go first. Then you, Tito, and you last, Felita."

Johnny went in for a little while, then Tito. Finally it was my turn.

"Felita"—Mami looked at me—"remember what I said to you." Boy, I thought, there she goes again.

I went and sat down beside Abuelita on her bed. She took my hand.

"How are you, Felita?"

"I'm really fine, Abuelita."

"You are? That's wonderful." She smiled. "Tell me about school and what you are doing with your friends."

I told Abuelita all about school. And about my friends.

"You and Gigi are still good friends, eh?" she asked.

"Yes, we are. Only one thing, Abuelita, Paquito isn't hanging out with us anymore."

"Is that so? Why?"

Then I remembered what Mami had said. I could feel myself blushing with embarrassment. I shouldn't be telling her, I thought.

"Go on." Abuelita smiled.

"Oh, it's nothing."

"Of course it's not nothing. That Paquito is not playing with you. Don't you want to confide in your abuelita anymore?"

"Yes, but . . ."

"But?"

"Well, Mami said . . ." I hesitated.

"What did your mother say? Go on."

"Well, she said I shouldn't tell you my troubles now."

"Rosa means well, but she's wrong. I want to hear your troubles. Yes, very much. Do you know why?" I shook my head. "Because when I help you solve your problems, it makes me feel smarter. And anytime I feel smarter, I feel better." She laughed, and then I laughed.

"Now, tell me all about Paquito."

"Well, he used to be so nice. Now he's just like the other boys. Such a pest! Like, he's teasing us all the time. And he doesn't want to play the games we used to play: you know, like hide-and-go-seek. When he does play, he has to be in charge. He's the youngest of all of us, and he wants to be in charge! And then he brings his dumb friends Aldo and Ernesto. They all try to boss us. I tell you, Abuelita, he's really changed."

"Could be Paquito got tired of being the only boy in your crowd."

"It never bothered him before."

"Well, but he's getting older. Maybe his interests are changing."

"I think it's dumb!"

"You don't like him anymore?"

"I still like him a little. But he's beginning to get on our nerves. Like just yesterday, him, Aldo, and Ernesto thought it was funny to pull Consuela's hair. It wasn't funny, you know. It hurt her. And before that they took one of Gigi's gloves and ran away. We had to chase them for blocks and blocks before they gave it back."

"You know, Felita, it could be that you will have to play less and less with Paquito. Maybe not play with him at all for a while."

"If he is gonna act like that, who cares? I'm not missing him. Neither is Gigi or Consuela."

"Don't worry, you and the other girls will be good friends with Paquito. It will just take some time."

"You think so, Abuelita?"

"Yes, when you are all older you will be friends again."

"Really?"

"Absolutely." Abuelita smiled. "I guarantee it." Her eyes were very bright. All the lines in her face seemed even deeper than before. "Give me a hug," she said.

I hugged her and she held me for a long, long time. "You are such a joy to me," she whispered. "Already you have made me feel much better."

"Abuelita, are you coming back soon from the hospital?"

"Of course I am. Remember that trip we are taking to Puerto Rico? We have to pick wild flowers in the countryside. You haven't forgotten, have you?"

"No." I smiled. "Abuelita, you make me real happy too."

I did not see my abuelita again after that last visit. She went to the hospital but she never returned home; my abuelita died at the end of spring. I felt sorriest for Papi. He loved his mother very much. He was sad and hardly spoke to anyone for many, many days after the funeral.

At first Mami was worried about Tío Jorge and how he would manage all alone. But now it was agreed that we were going to move into a larger apartment so that Tío Jorge could live with us. I was happy about that.

It felt strange to think that Abuelita was dead. I just found it hard to believe. I thought of the time those girls were mean to me in the new neighborhood. Mami had comforted me and spoken to me. But it was Abuelita who made me understand what Mami meant. She just knew how I felt and when I was sad. All my life she had been there when I needed her. There had always been my abuelita. Now she was no more.

On Sunday Tío Jorge took me to the park. He was quiet today, and he didn't tell me any stories. We were both quiet. I think we each knew how much we would miss Abuelita.

All the trees were wearing their brand-new leaves. Some of the branches were sprouting young flower buds. The new grass was a bright green.

"Tío Jorge, are you going to Puerto Rico?"

"You mean, to stay?" he asked.

"No, for a trip," I answered.

"What makes you ask that?"

"Abuelita and I were planning to go together."

"Is that so?"

"Yes. We talked about it . . . just before . . . before, you know."

"Well, I might go for a visit. Would you like to go with me, Felita?" I nodded. "Maybe we can go. We'll see."

"Are there many flowers there, like Abuelita said?"

"Oh, many, many flowers. They are everywhere you look."

We went on walking and then we stopped and sat on a high boulder overlooking a meadow.

I wondered if Abuelita could see me. Or was thinking of me. I knew I would always think of her. No matter how long I lived or how old I got, even if I got older than Abuelita. Silently I spoke to her. Abuelita, I said, when I go to Puerto Rico, I'm going to find the countryside you told me about. I'll pick lots of wild flowers. All the ones I can find, and in every color. I'll make a big bouquet, Abuelita. It will be just for you.